# Princess Truly

## and

# the hungry bunny problem

## by Kelly Greenawalt

Printed in the United States of America

Second Edition
First Printing, 2012

Published in the United States by Lemon Starfish Publishing

ISBN-10:1943806004
ISBN-13:978-1-943806-00-3

Library of Congress Control Number:  2015946042

The text of this book is set in 15pt Minion Pro font.
The illustrations in this book were created using watercolor and charcoal.
Visit us on the web at www.lemonstarfish.com

For Kitty and Moo. Momma loves you. ~ K.G.

For Junie and JJ ~ A.R.

This is Princess Truly. She lives at the tippy top of a tall tower with her snuggly pug Sir Noodles. Princess Truly has curly black hair that is puffy like a cloud and full of magic. She also has a very loving heart.

She reads many books, asks many questions and is especially good at solving problems. People from all over the land come to ask the princess for help because she is such a clever girl.

One warm and sunny summer afternoon, Princess Truly and
Sir Noodles were playing outside near the tower when the
princess heard a very sad sigh.

"Did you make that sad sigh, Sir Noodles?" asked the little
princess.

Sir Noodles shook his wrinkly head from side to side. It most
certainly was not his sigh.

But where did it come from? Princess Truly decided to
investigate and a curious Sir Noodles decided to follow
her. Just beyond the tower, they found a very sad Lola Little.

Lola was a gentle girl that loved animals, especially rabbits.
In fact, some of her best friends were bunnies. One
bunny in particular followed her everywhere she went and
his name was Bun. Bun's favorite past time was eating and
his favorite person was Lola. Mostly because she fed him lots
of crunchy carrots, but also because she always rubbed behind
his long white ears.

"Good afternoon Lola, why are you so sad?" asked the princess.

"I planted carrots," said Lola sniffling,"and they will not grow.
 If the carrots do not grow, I can not feed my hungry bunnies."

"Oh goodness," said Princess Truly, "that is very troubling news."

"Can you help me solve my hungry bunny problem?" asked Lola.

"I would be happy to help," beamed the little princess. "And so would Sir Noodles."

huh?

Sir Noodles raised his wrinkly eyebrow. He was sleepy but he supposed he could help.

Bun was so excited his little nose twitchy-twitched and he hopped right over to Sir Noodles to thank him.

boing
boing
boing

slurp!

Sir Noodle's long slurpy tongue fell out of his slobbery mouth and he licked the little white rabbit. Instantly they were friends.

And so they set off. Princess Truly and Lola Little walked hand in hand. Bun hopped beside them and Sir Noodles waddled behind them. They crossed Crickety Creek.

Passed under the giant oak.

And looked both ways before crossing Dusty Road. Finally they arrived at Lola's garden.

Sir Noodles, who was exhausted from the long journey, found a shady spot under the apple tree where he could rest. Bun sat down beside him.

"This is my garden," said Lola. "And here is where I planted the carrot seeds that will not grow."

"I see," said the princess. "There is not a single carrot."

"And my bunny is so hungry," said Lola.

"I once read a book that taught me about gardening," said Princess Truly. "I learned that in order for vegetables to grow they need lots of sunshine, plenty of water and fertile soil - which is a fancy name for good dirt."

"Plenty of water? Oh rats! I forgot to water the seeds!" said
Lola Little.

"We may have found the problem then," said the Princess.

"But how will we solve it," wondered Lola.

"Do you have a bucket?" asked the princess.

Lola most certainly did. Princess Truly explained that they could use the bucket to fetch water down at Crickety Creek.

And so they set off...

They looked both ways when they crossed Dusty Road. They passed under the giant oak and carefully walked to the bank of Crickety Creek to fill Lola's bucket with water. When the bucket was full to the very top, they skipped back to the garden.

ah uh ah uh

Unfortunately they skipped so swiftly that they did not notice that the bucket was empty until they reached the garden.

"Oh rats!" cried Lola "The bucket is empty!"

"There appears to be a hole in the bucket. Unfortunately our solution has a problem of its own," said the princess.

"Yes," agreed Lola, who was starting to feel less hopeful and much sadder.

"Sniffly Sniff," added Bun, who was starting to feel much hungrier.

Princess Truly did her very best thinking when she snuggled her pug. So she sat down beside Sir Noodles. She rubbed his soft, velvety ears and kissed his wrinkly head.

"Thinkety, think," she said out loud which made Lola giggle.

"Peep! Thinkety! Peep!" said a little bird in the apple tree as she fluffed and fluttered nearly falling off the branch.

"Oh! Little blue bird, that is a fantastic idea! I need to fluff and flutter," said Princess Truly.

"I am very confused," said Lola Little.

"I suppose I do need to explain," said the princess.

"A long time ago, when I was just a baby princess, a ray of sunshine reached down from the sky and got caught in my curly hair. It swirled and twirled. It gleamed and it glowed. It sparkled and it shined," said the princess.

"And then?" said Lola.

"And then my curly hair was full of magic," said Princess
Truly. "Sometimes when I have a problem, my hair has an
extra special solution."

"We sure need an extra special solution!" said Lola.

Princess Truly fluffed and shook her magical puffy hair. Her curls twisted and sparkled. They gleamed and they glowed. The wind began to swirl and twirl. It whipped and it whistled. It bustled and blustered and blew. Bun's little bunny nose twitched with excitement. And then the sunny sky was filled with the most peculiar purple clouds.

"Something truly magical is happening," said Lola.

"Truly!" said the little blue bird.

"Ow wow wooo!" barked Sir Noodles.

And just then, water began to fall from the peculiar purple clouds in the sky. Big fat rain drops plopped on the fertile soil. Little bitty rain drops danced all over the garden. This was no ordinary rain. It was full of magic. And soon the garden was full of little green sprouts. It rained and rained. The sprouts grew and grew. And before their eyes, giant crunchy carrots appeared.

"Oh wow!" said Lola.

"Peep!" said the little blue bird.

"What an extraordinary rain!" said Princess Truly.

"Now all bunnies will have plenty to eat," said Lola.

Bun shared some of his carrots with his friend, Sir Noodles.

crunch
crunch
munch

Sir Noodles made a funny face. He decided that pugs do not like carrots very much even though they are the same color as yummy cheese.

Because of Princess Truly and her magic hair there was never another hungry bunny in the land again. Lola Little and her bunny friends thanked the soggy princess and waved goodbye as Princess Truly and Sir Noodles set off for their tower.

Made in the USA
Middletown, DE
21 October 2016